Acting Edition

Kodachrome

One-Act Version

by Adam Szymkowicz

Copyright © 2022 by Adam Szymkowicz
All Rights Reserved

KODACHROME (ONE-ACT VERSION) is fully protected under the copyright laws of the United States of America, the British Commonwealth, including Canada, and all member countries of the Berne Convention for the Protection of Literary and Artistic Works, the Universal Copyright Convention, and/or the World Trade Organization conforming to the Agreement on Trade Related Aspects of Intellectual Property Rights. All rights, including professional and amateur stage productions, recitation, lecturing, public reading, motion picture, radio broadcasting, television, online/digital production, and the rights of translation into foreign languages are strictly reserved.

ISBN 978-0-573-70982-1

www.concordtheatricals.com
www.concordtheatricals.co.uk

FOR PRODUCTION INQUIRIES

UNITED STATES AND CANADA
info@concordtheatricals.com
1-866-979-0447

UNITED KINGDOM AND EUROPE
licensing@concordtheatricals.co.uk
020-7054-7298

Each title is subject to availability from Concord Theatricals Corp., depending upon country of performance. Please be aware that *KODACHROME (ONE-ACT VERSION)* may not be licensed by Concord Theatricals Corp. in your territory. Professional and amateur producers should contact the nearest Concord Theatricals Corp. office or licensing partner to verify availability.

CAUTION: Professional and amateur producers are hereby warned that *KODACHROME (ONE-ACT VERSION)* is subject to a licensing fee. The purchase, renting, lending or use of this book does not constitute a license to perform this title(s), which license must be obtained from Concord Theatricals Corp. prior to any performance. Performance of this title(s) without a license is a violation of federal law and may subject the producer and/or presenter of such performances to civil penalties. Both amateurs and professionals considering a production are strongly advised to apply to the appropriate agent before starting rehearsals, advertising, or booking a theatre. A licensing fee must be paid whether the title(s) is presented for charity or gain and whether or not admission is charged. Professional/Stock licensing fees are quoted upon application to Concord Theatricals Corp.

This work is published by Samuel French, an imprint of Concord Theatricals Corp.

No one shall make any changes in this title(s) for the purpose of production. No part of this book may be reproduced, stored in a retrieval system, scanned, uploaded, or transmitted in any form, by any means, now known or yet to be invented, including mechanical, electronic, digital, photocopying, recording, videotaping, or otherwise, without the prior written permission of the publisher. No one shall share this title(s), or any part of this title(s), through any social media or file hosting websites.

For all inquiries regarding motion picture, television, online/digital and other media rights, please contact Concord Theatricals Corp.

MUSIC AND THIRD-PARTY MATERIALS USE NOTE

Licensees are solely responsible for obtaining formal written permission from copyright owners to use copyrighted music and/or other copyrighted third-party materials (e.g. artworks, logos) in the performance of this play and are strongly cautioned to do so. If no such permission is obtained by the licensee, then the licensee must use only original music and materials that the licensee owns and controls. Licensees are solely responsible and liable for clearances of all third-party copyrighted materials, including without limitation music, and shall indemnify the copyright owners of the play(s) and their licensing agent, Concord Theatricals Corp., against any costs, expenses, losses and liabilities arising from the use of such copyrighted third-party materials by licensees. For music, please contact the appropriate music licensing authority in your territory for the rights to any incidental music.

IMPORTANT BILLING AND CREDIT REQUIREMENTS

If you have obtained performance rights to this title, please refer to your licensing agreement for important billing and credit requirements.

KODACHROME was originally developed in the Dorothy Strelsin New American Writers Group at Primary Stages in New York, New York. It was workshopped at JAW: A Playwrights Festival, produced by Portland Center Stage in Portland, Oregon in 2015.

CHARACTERS

5-13 total.
As few as 3 women, 2 men with doubling
or as many as 7 women, 4 men, 2 any gender without doubling.
Actors can be any race.

THE PHOTOGRAPHER – Suzanne, female, mid-thirties to mid-forties.

THE GRAVEDIGGER – Earl, male, mid-thirties to mid-forties.

THE HARDWARE STORE OWNER – Charlie, male, mid-thirties to mid-forties.

THE HISTORY PROFESSOR – Harold, male, early sixties.

THE MYSTERY NOVELIST – Georgette, female, early sixties.

MARJORY – female, mid-twenties.

THE YOUNG MAN – Robert, male, early twenties.

THE YOUNG WOMAN – Florence, female, early twenties.

FRIEND – female, early twenties.

EMT 1

EMT 2

THE LIBRARIAN – Renee, female, mid-thirties to mid-forties.

THE FLORIST – Heather, female.

SETTING

Colchester, Connecticut
a small rural New England town.

TIME

The present or recent past

DOUBLING FOR 5

The Photographer

Gravedigger / Young Man

Hardware Store Owner / History Professor / EMT 1

Mystery Novelist / The Librarian / The Florist / Friend / EMT 2

Young Woman / Marjory

NOTE ABOUT PROJECTIONS

These are not entirely necessary. I think The Photographer showing the audience is also effective in an *Our Town* kind of way. Which is to say please don't be daunted by the projections. They are nice but entirely unnecessary.

If you do projections, I suggest the photos taken onstage be taken beforehand in actual locations like an actual diner or an actual library so there's a richness that you won't be able to get from an onstage photo.

For the photos of the audience, in Portland, the actress had a wireless video transmitter connected to her camera and concealed in her costume. They used a program called Isadora to "watch" the video feed from the camera, and output individual frames of the feed to a projector as the actress took photos. They found that outputting a video feed from the camera and capturing images on the computer eliminated the delay incurred by outputting images from the camera directly. Again, if that seems daunting, just have her take photos which aren't projected.

NOTE

If this version still runs a little too long for your purposes, you are welcome to cut Scene Eight or Scene Ten, or both.

For the many teachers who have changed my life, especially Liz Bochain, the late Franklin S. Gross, Tish Dace, Eduardo Machado, Kelly Stuart, Marsha Norman, Chris Durang, Kristen Palmer, John Szymkowicz, Rhoda Szymkowicz.

Scene One
"The Photographer"

(Photos projected on the rear wall of the inhabitants and environs of a small town. But something is a little off. A little odd. The color saturated and too dark. The camera too close. Unusual perspective. Things like that.)

(During the slideshow, **THE PHOTOGRAPHER** *enters. She is in all white or in muted colors and she wears a camera around her neck. She smiles at us.)*

PHOTOGRAPHER. I have loved! – No. Let me start again.

(Beat.)

I take photos. It's important, I think to record things. So I take a lot of photos of everywhere and everyone here in town. I'm not an official photographer although there are political grumblings from time to time to that effect. Does a town need an official photographer? Or an official poet? An official dreamer? An official lover? I don't need to be the official photographer. But I am good at it. People always come to me for keepsakes, or for help remembering. Course I'm having a bit of trouble remembering now too. Little things. It's one of the side effects of my condition. I'm getting ahead of myself. I take photos. I can't stop time so instead I – I have photos up in a lot of public spaces. For historical record. For art, maybe. I don't know if it's art. You can call me Suzanne. Or The Photographer. Hold on. *(Raises her camera to her eye, takes photos.)* Stay still. Yeah. Turn your head just. You're very photogenic.

1

You too. Show me your sadness. Good. A smile? A sad smile. Now joy. Great! Can you button that up?

> (**THE PHOTOGRAPHER** *takes a bunch of photos of the audience. They appear on the screen behind her.*)

Good. That's great. I want to remember this. Maybe you will too. Where to first? Our time is limited.

> (*Lights on* **YOUNG WOMAN** *and* **YOUNG MAN.**)

The Young Man thinks about the Young Woman. The Young Woman thinks about the Young Man.

> (*They steal a glance. Lights out on* **YOUNG WOMAN** *and* **YOUNG MAN.**)

> (*Spot on the* **LIBRARIAN**, *walking.*)

The Librarian walks by the hardware store on the way to the library. She wills herself not to look in the window.

LIBRARIAN. I will not.

> (*Lights up on* **HARDWARE STORE OWNER** *with pipe.*)

PHOTOGRAPHER. The Hardware Store Owner does not see her walk by. He is measuring a length of pipe and trying not to think about the hole in the center of him he hasn't been able to fill.

HARDWARE STORE OWNER. And seven eighths.

> (*Spot on* **GRAVEDIGGER.**)

PHOTOGRAPHER. The Gravedigger looks at the sky and wonders if it will rain.

GRAVEDIGGER. I wonder if it will rain.

PHOTOGRAPHER. He scans the gravestones looking for ghosts, but he sees none.

> (**GRAVEDIGGER** *sighs.* **THE PHOTOGRAPHER** *takes a photo and it is projected on the back wall. Lights on* **HISTORY PROFESSOR** *and* **MYSTERY NOVELIST.** *She is writing while walking. He is reading.*)

The History Professor and the Mystery Novelist both enter the kitchen at the same time from different directions. They both reach for the coffee pot.

HISTORY PROFESSOR. You go ahead.

MYSTERY NOVELIST. No, no. You.

HISTORY PROFESSOR. I insist.

> (*They freeze. Lights out on them.*)

> (**THE FLORIST** *enters.*)

PHOTOGRAPHER. The Florist opens her Flower Shop.

FLORIST. Another day.

PHOTOGRAPHER. She is optimistic.

FLORIST. I think. Yes. I think. Why not?

> (**THE PHOTOGRAPHER** *takes a photo which is projected.*)

> (*Lights up on* **THE LIBRARIAN.**)

PHOTOGRAPHER. When The Librarian stops in the grocery store before lunch, there The Hardware Store Owner is, looking at radishes.

> (*Spot on* **HARDWARE STORE OWNER,** *examining a radish.*)

She ducks behind the heads of lettuce.

*(*LIBRARIAN *hides.* THE PHOTOGRAPHER *takes a photo and it is projected on the back wall. Lights on* YOUNG WOMAN *and* YOUNG MAN.*)*

The Young Man thinks about the Young Woman. The Young Woman thinks about the Young Man.

(They steal a glance. Lights out on YOUNG WOMAN *and* YOUNG MAN.*)*

Scene Two
"The History Professor and The Mystery Novelist"

  (Photo of Harry's Place appears. An older couple sit at a picnic table or rustic outdoor table, **THE HISTORY PROFESSOR** *and* **THE MYSTERY NOVELIST.***)*

PHOTOGRAPHER. Harry's Place, established nineteen twenty. Drive in, take out, affordable hot dogs, burgers and fries. The History Professor and The Mystery Novelist sit in the shade. It's a mild August afternoon. The History Professor fiddles with his wedding ring.

HISTORY PROFESSOR. So.

PHOTOGRAPHER. He says.

MYSTERY NOVELIST. Yes.

PHOTOGRAPHER. She says.

  She takes a bite from her lobster roll. Butter drips down her chin.

HISTORY PROFESSOR. I'll have it all drawn up.

PHOTOGRAPHER. She smiles at this, a small smile. A slight breeze. They watch a hummingbird pass.

  *(***PHOTOGRAPHER** *takes a photo of her, projected on the back wall.)*

MYSTERY NOVELIST. I do appreciate of course, your sense of humor.

HISTORY PROFESSOR. Humor?

MYSTERY NOVELIST. Irony. Finality. History? I see how you are rounding it out, putting up book ends as it were.

HISTORY PROFESSOR. Our first date.

MYSTERY NOVELIST. Yes. You wore a letter jacket. How did you ever letter in anything?

HISTORY PROFESSOR. It was out of pity. You were cold. Wearing a tiny dress. I draped it over you.

PHOTOGRAPHER. They settle into an unsettled silence. That was then. But now – Now –

HISTORY PROFESSOR. I'll move into the cottage.

MYSTERY NOVELIST. No, no.

HISTORY PROFESSOR. I insist.

PHOTOGRAPHER. He says goodbye in his mind to his oak bookcase and the red couch in his study. She feels the pull of the novel she's writing. How to get her heroine out of the water. Do boats just come along? Does she float for a while? Was she perhaps a champion swimmer? Reminds herself to look up how long it takes for hypothermia to set in. Instead what she says is

MYSTERY NOVELIST. What will we tell the kids?

HISTORY PROFESSOR. Jonathan will take it in stride. But Marjory. I worry about Marjory.

PHOTOGRAPHER. She doesn't tell him that Marjory already knows. Over the phone. Last week. Marjory pleaded. Marjory cried.

(**MARJORY** *appears in spot, in pain.*)

MARJORY. Mother, please. Don't do this. Are you fighting? I don't understand.

MYSTERY NOVELIST. I long for an empty bed. I want to drink coffee alone in the morning. I want to be lonely.

MARJORY. Is he having an affair? Are you?

MYSTERY NOVELIST. No. No. I want him to move out before I begin to hate him. His toenails. His breath. The grunty way he stands up.

MARJORY. Don't do this. Please!

MYSTERY NOVELIST. We will be civil when we see you. We will come visit together maybe. How's your roommate?

PHOTOGRAPHER. And Marjory is distracted for twenty minutes talking about the trials of life in Boston and the HR game.

MARJORY. Do you think I'm ambitious enough? Sometimes I can't tell the difference between what I want and what I think I should want. What do you think?

PHOTOGRAPHER. And then she becomes aware of how dull she must sound to her mother. Her mother admires her daughter with her feet on the ground, but then there never is the clouds of the mind to discuss. But The Mystery Novelist asks questions to show she is listening. Like –

MYSTERY NOVELIST. How is the transition to the new software? How did you feel about last quarter?

PHOTOGRAPHER. And Marjory knows her mother is trying. Did she try in her marriage? Marjory cries and pleads and cries.

MARJORY. Nooooooo!

PHOTOGRAPHER. She feels sorry for herself and imagines she now comes from a broken home. She looks at the bean bag chair and remembers when her parents helped her move in. She makes microwave popcorn and falls asleep to *Casablanca*.

(**MARJORY** *exits. Light change.*)

MYSTERY NOVELIST. I'll tell Marjory.

PHOTOGRAPHER. She says to her still husband. And a weight he didn't know was there is lifted off his shoulders.

HISTORY PROFESSOR. I'll say something to Jonathan.

PHOTOGRAPHER. And like that, the plan becomes all too very real.

Scene Three
"The Young Couple"

(The Town Green. Behind **THE YOUNG MAN** *and* **THE YOUNG WOMAN**, *photo of the gazebo.)*

PHOTOGRAPHER. The Young Couple go for a stroll. She does not realize it is more than a stroll. But she senses something stirring in him, unfamiliar. He is upset perhaps, anxious. This makes her nervous. Is he angry at her? Did she speak too sharply earlier when she was hungry and irritable? He is unaware of the tempest in her mind. He has an important question to ask. He reaches into his pocket to feel the ring box. By trickery he got her best friend to find out her ring size.

FRIEND. *(Appears in spot, a ring in her hand.)* Try this one on. That looks good on you.

PHOTOGRAPHER. The Young Woman did not suspect. Even now, she thinks his silence means the opposite. He is done with her, she thinks. She has always suspected she was not one of those girls who could be loved.

YOUNG MAN. Florence –

PHOTOGRAPHER. He says.

YOUNG MAN. Florence.

PHOTOGRAPHER. She waits for more but the words get stuck in him. She waits for him to say. "It's not working out," or "We're just too different." "I love you but sometimes love isn't enough." Or something like that. She doesn't know he really wants to say, "I love you madly." "I want to marry you." "Let's spend our lives together." Or something along those lines. He is having trouble getting the words out. His throat constricts.

YOUNG MAN. ... ...

YOUNG WOMAN. Are you okay?

YOUNG MAN. …

PHOTOGRAPHER. The Young Man begins to hyperventilate. He falls to one knee, thinking she will understand. *(Takes photo which is projected.)*

YOUNG WOMAN. What is wrong? Can you breathe? Are you allergic to something? Did you swallow something?

YOUNG MAN. …

PHOTOGRAPHER. She calls nine-one-one.

YOUNG WOMAN. *(Into phone.)* Something is wrong. Something is terribly wrong.

> (**YOUNG MAN** *collapses. She goes to him.*)

PHOTOGRAPHER. He is unconscious when the EMTs arrive.

> (**EMT**s *check vitals, give him oxygen.*)

EMT 1. What was he doing right before?

YOUNG WOMAN. I don't know. He fell to one knee. He was breathing too fast.

> (**EMT 1** *and* **EMT 2** *nod sagely to one another.*)

EMT 1. I've seen this before. Sir can you hear me?

YOUNG MAN. Eh…anh…

EMT 2. Shall I check your pocket sir?

PHOTOGRAPHER. The Young Man nods to the EMT.

> (**EMT 2** *takes the ring box from his pocket, gives it to* **YOUNG WOMAN.***)*

EMT 2. I believe this is for you.

PHOTOGRAPHER. It gets eerily quiet as The Young Woman has eight separate feelings. One. Two. Three. Four. Five. Six. Seven. Eight.

YOUNG WOMAN. I – I –

(The **YOUNG WOMAN** *throws her arms around the* **YOUNG MAN.***)*

EMT 1. I think that's a yes.

PHOTOGRAPHER. The Young Man finds his voice again. It had been in the ring box the whole time.

YOUNG MAN. Florence! Will you –

YOUNG WOMAN. Yes, Robert. Of course, yes.

(She takes the oxygen mask off and kisses him.)

PHOTOGRAPHER. Young Love. Mmm.

Scene Four
"The Gravedigger and The Hardware Store Owner"

(**PHOTOGRAPHER** *in spot.*)

PHOTOGRAPHER. I have to – I have some errands. Here is the graveyard. It all comes back here, doesn't it? We try to avoid it, don't we? Anyway – The Hardware Store Owner.

(**PHOTOGRAPHER** *exits. A graveyard photo appears on the back wall.* **THE HARDWARE STORE OWNER** *stands by a grave. He looks down at it, dour. Says nothing.*)

HARDWARE STORE OWNER. So. Um. So. Sometimes it's hard to start. But I don't know how. So. Um.

(**THE GRAVEDIGGER** *enters, stands beside him.*)

GRAVEDIGGER. You didn't bring flowers.

HARDWARE STORE OWNER. They just die.

GRAVEDIGGER. Oh but. Sure but. Why is that a problem? I have some. I could put down some for her, make her part of the rotation.

HARDWARE STORE OWNER. I'll bring some next time.

GRAVEDIGGER. Sometimes I get the leftover ones from the florist. Before they die but at the end of the day. She likes flowers doesn't she? I think she likes flowers.

HARDWARE STORE OWNER. The florist?

GRAVEDIGGER. No.

(*Beat.*)

You want a minute? Sometimes people want a minute but they don't know how to tell me.

HARDWARE STORE OWNER. I have to go anyway.

GRAVEDIGGER. I'll let her know you stopped by.

HARDWARE STORE OWNER. Okay. Okay, Earl. Thanks. Tell your mother I said "Hi."

GRAVEDIGGER. I will do that. I will. Looks like I might have to cut the grass early this week. But maybe I'll wait. Lunch. Maybe I'll have lunch. What time is it? Is it too early?

HARDWARE STORE OWNER. Okay, Earl. You take care.

(HARDWARE STORE OWNER *exits.*)

GRAVEDIGGER. I don't care if it is too early.

(**GRAVEDIGGER** *gets a cooler/lunchbox. He sits down and starts eating.* **THE PHOTOGRAPHER** *appears.*)

There you are. He was just here. Your husband.

PHOTOGRAPHER. My widower. He's harder to remember. His edges are fuzzy. Does he seem like he's fading to you?

GRAVEDIGGER. He was hoping to talk to you I think. But he can't hear you. Not like me. I'm going to pick up some flowers for your grave tomorrow. Is there a particular kind you like or don't like?

PHOTOGRAPHER. Peonies?

GRAVEDIGGER. I don't know what that is.

PHOTOGRAPHER. I will treasure whatever you get.

GRAVEDIGGER. You don't mind that they die?

PHOTOGRAPHER. No. Everything dies.

GRAVEDIGGER. Yeah, I don't know why that would be a problem either. I really like spending so much time with you. I like having you around I mean. It's been – I'm not good with words, but –

PHOTOGRAPHER. I know. It's nice to talk to you too.

GRAVEDIGGER. Right. That's all I meant. It's been nice. But you know, eventually, one of these days, you will have to move on. It's the natural way and I don't know about a lot of things but I know about the natural way. Say what you have to say to him and then, well, I'll miss you of course and all. Does this grass look long to you?

> *(She looks at it. He takes out a tape measure and measures the grass. She takes a photo of him. He freezes. She talks to us.)*

PHOTOGRAPHER. I'm sorry I didn't mention before I was dead. Does it matter too much to you? I still have a perspective.

Scene Five
"The Florist and The Young Woman"

(Projected: Interior of a Flower Shop. The **YOUNG WOMAN** *looks at a binder of bridal bouquets. The* **FLORIST** *stands nearby.)*

PHOTOGRAPHER. The Young Woman is not someone to waste time. Here she is picking out her bridal bouquet.

YOUNG WOMAN. Not this one. No. No. No. It must feel inevitable. It must feel like forever.

PHOTOGRAPHER. The Florist is always a little misty when the brides come in. Each year they get younger and younger and the Florist gets older and older.

FLORIST. It doesn't matter. It's fine.

PHOTOGRAPHER. And a wave of anxiety overtakes her. What if? What if not? What if tomorrow? What if never?

FLORIST. Do you have a color scheme?

YOUNG WOMAN. I just want perfection.

PHOTOGRAPHER. The Young Woman is feeling constricted. She is having trouble breathing. The Young Woman does not understand the tides within her, the eight separate emotions that change into eight other slightly different emotions. One Two Three Four Five Six Seven Eight. One Two Three Four Five Six Seven Eight.

YOUNG WOMAN. Are these all the options?

FLORIST. There's another book.

YOUNG WOMAN. I need to see all the books. If it can't be perfect, why do it at all?

FLORIST. Love?

YOUNG WOMAN. What?

FLORIST. Because of love.

YOUNG WOMAN. Love. Love. It just has to start the right way. What if – do you have suggestions?

FLORIST. Of course. What would you like?

YOUNG WOMAN. No. No. No. You're not helping me at all. I need to get some fresh air!

PHOTOGRAPHER. The Florist has seen this before and is unfazed. The Young Woman runs out of the flower shop. She has never felt this way before. Outside she doesn't feel any better. The Florist feels immediately better.

YOUNG WOMAN. I will go to a different Flower Shop.

PHOTOGRAPHER. The Young Woman thinks of the anti-anxiety pills in the very back of her sock drawer. But why should she need this, now at the happiest moment of her life? The Florist smiles with a renewed optimism. The flowers die a little with every passing second.

Scene Six
"The Librarian and The Young Man"

(Photo of exterior of library on the back wall.)

PHOTOGRAPHER. Cragin Memorial Library, built 1905, a fine example of early twentieth-century Neoclassical architecture.

(Photo of interior of library. **THE LIBRARIAN** *looks up at a light that has gone out.)*

The Librarian looks up at the lightbulb that has gone out.

LIBRARIAN. Darn.

PHOTOGRAPHER. It's easy enough for her to put in an order. But there is an account at the hardware store and it's important to support small businesses. She has been meaning to stop and say hello to the Hardware Store Owner. She's been intending to do so for the last two years. She imagines how easy it would be to walk through those doors. This is the part of her that imagines a braver version of herself. Tomorrow she will be thinner, the lines will disappear from her face, she will clean the bathroom thoroughly and she will go to the hardware store. But why not now? Every day it's tomorrow and tomorrow and tomorrow.

LIBRARIAN. Tomorrow.

PHOTOGRAPHER. She's been tomorrowing in one way or another for the past twenty years. Best not to think about it. And then the Young Man appears.

YOUNG MAN. Hello.

PHOTOGRAPHER. He says.

YOUNG MAN. I'm wondering if you could help me. I'm looking for a book.

LIBRARIAN. You've come to the right place.

YOUNG MAN. I am looking for books on marriage. How to have a good marriage. What to do. What not to do. How to be a good husband. How to love the right way. How to best make love. Not fiction, mind you. Or the things on the internet. More like old knowledge. The things our souls know that long ago were shared by word of mouth generation after generation and then recorded by hand and translated into a thousand languages but have been forgotten. Also. How to be a good father. How to be a good person. How to live life the right way. I feel like I'm trying to start my life finally with the right person and I want to try not to make too many mistakes and I want to be happy or if not happy, the other thing that we're supposed to be. Of use? Worthwhile? Honest? I want to be vulnerable and love completely. Do you have a book like that?

PHOTOGRAPHER. The Librarian is quietly astonished by the Young Man.

LIBRARIAN. I should be more like him.

PHOTOGRAPHER. He worries he has said too much. While he worries, she hands him a stack of books.

> (THE PHOTOGRAPHER *takes a photo as the* YOUNG MAN *accepts the stack of books from the* LIBRARIAN. *It is projected.*)

YOUNG MAN. I really appreciate it. Really – I thanks!

> (YOUNG MAN *exits with a large stack of books.*)

> (PHOTOGRAPHER *takes a photo of* LIBRARIAN *which is projected.*)

LIBRARIAN. Vulnerable. Love Completely. Well. Well.

PHOTOGRAPHER. She feels something rising in her. She will not tomorrow today. She will today today. She takes a deep breath. She steels herself. And she puts one foot after another towards the hardware store where my former husband is right then ordering hammers.

(**LIBRARIAN** *exits.*)

Scene Seven
"The Librarian and The Hardware Store Owner"

(Photo of the interior of the Hardware Store projected. **HARDWARE STORE OWNER** *is there working.* **THE PHOTOGRAPHER** *enters.)*

PHOTOGRAPHER. If I'm honest, I have to admit I've been avoiding this place. The Hardware Store. The Librarian lurks outside.

(Enter **LIBRARIAN** *who lurks.)*

LIBRARIAN. It's just a lightbulb. It's no big deal.

PHOTOGRAPHER. She reaches for the door handle. The Hardware Store Owner looks up. Their eyes meet.

HARDWARE STORE OWNER. Oh.

LIBRARIAN. I –

HARDWARE STORE OWNER. Renee.

LIBRARIAN. Charlie.

(They are frozen.)

PHOTOGRAPHER. She should have expected this. But then – there is history, isn't there.

(A mirrored ball is lowered from the ceiling. Music. Lights change. The* **HARDWARE STORE OWNER** *and* **THE LIBRARIAN** *come together. They slow dance.)*

The prom theme was "Parisian Nights." The prom song was "In Your Eyes," by Mr. Peter Gabriel. She thinks

---

* A license to produce *Kodachrome (One-Act Version)* does not include a performance license for any third-party or copyrighted music. Licensees should create an original composition or use music in the public domain. For further information, please see the Music and Third Party Materials Use Note on page iii.

about the future. Their colleges are not so far away. Weekends together. And then, graduation, marriage, children. She thinks of names for their kids.

LIBRARIAN. Sophie. Liz. Margaret.

PHOTOGRAPHER. He thinks about later that night. He must be careful. There is a basketball scholarship on the line. College is the way out, the way to say no to the family business. What does he know about screws, drills, viscosity.

HARDWARE STORE OWNER. Nuts and bolts.

LIBRARIAN. This night is perfect.

HARDWARE STORE OWNER. Yes.

LIBRARIAN. I can't wait for everything that comes next and also I want it to just be now forever, you know what I mean?

PHOTOGRAPHER. He does know what she means. It seems like maybe, just maybe this moment will last forever.

> (**PHOTOGRAPHER** *takes a photo of them which is projected.*)

But it doesn't.

> (*The lights change.* **THE HARDWARE STORE OWNER** *and* **LIBRARIAN** *move away from one another. The present day awkwardness returns.*)

LIBRARIAN. Hello.

HARDWARE STORE OWNER. Long time no see.

LIBRARIAN. Busy over there at the library.

HARDWARE STORE OWNER. Here too. You know how it is. You wake up and wonder what day it is.

LIBRARIAN. What month.

HARDWARE STORE OWNER. What can I do for you?

PHOTOGRAPHER. Immediately he feels like he said too much.

HARDWARE STORE OWNER. I didn't mean to imply. A drill? A socket wrench? Nuts and bolts?

LIBRARIAN. Oh! Oh. Lightbulbs. For the Library.

HARDWARE STORE OWNER. Of course.

PHOTOGRAPHER. The Hardware Store Owner goes to the computer and looks up the type of lightbulbs the Library usually orders.

LIBRARIAN. Do you want the account number?

HARDWARE STORE OWNER. Sure.

PHOTOGRAPHER. He says, even though he has the account number memorized.

LIBRARIAN. *(Reading off a page.)* Zero Six Four One Five, Eight Six Zero, Two Zero Three, Eight, Six Seven Six Seven Seven Seven, Two Two One Five Three Eight Seven Two Three Nine One One Seven Six.

> *(You don't have to memorize this number. Keep saying numbers. If they laugh, say one more number after the laugh. If not, just stop eventually. Always end on one.)*

One. I like those lightbulbs.

HARDWARE STORE OWNER. They're really good. We sell them a lot.

PHOTOGRAPHER. This isn't really the conversation either of them wish they were having right now. How did we get here? Two weeks after the prom there was a fight.

> *(Lights change.* **THE LIBRARIAN** *and* **THE HARDWARE STORE OWNER** *fight.)*

Who can say what it was really about? Fear of the future. Loss of control. The problem of independent personalities.

LIBRARIAN. You're a stubborn jerk!

HARDWARE STORE OWNER. You're mean!

LIBRARIAN. Stop looking at me with those stupid eyes in that stupid face.

HARDWARE STORE OWNER. I wish I never had to deal with you ever again.

LIBRARIAN. Then maybe we should break up.

HARDWARE STORE OWNER. Maybe we should.

(Lights change.)

PHOTOGRAPHER. When I asked him out, he said yes to make her mad. Probably. I wasn't supposed to get pregnant. Definitely.

We got married right away. Quickly, quietly. Days turned to weeks. Weeks turned to love.

HARDWARE STORE OWNER. Love.

PHOTOGRAPHER. He turned down his scholarship. He took over the family business. The future Librarian went to college. And then my baby came and she was stillborn. We mourned. The future Librarian came back from college and got a job at the Library. And then life and life and life. Until four years ago when I came down with bone cancer and then two years ago when I stopped being alive.

(Lights. Back to present.)

LIBRARIAN. I've been meaning to stop by and say hi anyway.

HARDWARE STORE OWNER. Sure. Hi.

PHOTOGRAPHER. He can't find the words he needs because two years in the grave, I still have a hold on him.

She notices a photo of mine hanging behind him.

LIBRARIAN. That's a real nice shot. She was talented. I like how everyone's personality always comes through. And the personality of the buildings too. They all feel alive.

PHOTOGRAPHER. Even now that I'm dead. But she doesn't say that. She shouldn't have pointed out the photograph. She thinks of leaving the store, the state, the country. Instead she walks towards the fear. Steels herself. And she says –

LIBRARIAN. Tomorrow are you – might you want to have dinner with me. The new Italian place? Just dinner.

PHOTOGRAPHER. In the silence, everything they can't say is said.

(Light shift.)

HARDWARE STORE OWNER. I can't disrespect her memory. No matter what you think, it was love.

LIBRARIAN. There has never been anyone but you. Not really. Not anyone. I feel terrible but I was a little happy, just a little happy when I heard she died. I felt bad right after, but for a second –

(Light shift.)

HARDWARE STORE OWNER. I'm sorry. Things are just really busy now. Maybe another time.

PHOTOGRAPHER. The Librarian leaves, trying to not let him see her face.

(Exit LIBRARIAN.)

HARDWARE STORE OWNER. Wait! Your lightbulbs.

PHOTOGRAPHER. But she has gone.

Scene Eight
"The Florist and The Gravedigger"

(The interior of the Flower Shop is projected.
THE FLORIST *is there waiting on* **THE**
GRAVEDIGGER.)

PHOTOGRAPHER. The Gravedigger selects flowers.

GRAVEDIGGER. Yeah, like that except prettier.

FLORIST. Don't you just want the discards? For the graves?

GRAVEDIGGER. Today, I will buy some. I will spend money. Maybe I will spend a lot of money. Are they expensive?

FLORIST. Depends what you want and what you think expensive means.

GRAVEDIGGER. I have some money saved.

PHOTOGRAPHER. The Florist does not know what this means.

GRAVEDIGGER. I want to buy the most beautiful flowers you have. Which ones are those?

FLORIST. We all can't agree on that. If we all could agree on that, well, it would be a different world.

GRAVEDIGGER. Which do you like best? You're a woman. You might know.

FLORIST. You're buying them for someone special? Why don't you get what you like? And she'll know you better by it.

GRAVEDIGGER. She did say – do you have ponies?

FLORIST. No.

GRAVEDIGGER. It's just – how can she let go until I do? I have to show her. And she's stuck around longer than most but I see her fading. It won't be long now. Whether she wants to or not. So... Flowers like that.

PHOTOGRAPHER. Then he sees me.

GRAVEDIGGER. Shhh. Act normal.

FLORIST. How am I acting?

GRAVEDIGGER. *(Looking down.)* I'm just getting some flowers, like I always do. I want the biggest most beautiful bouquet you can make. Use all the flowers that mean nice things and that smell good.

FLORIST. Okay.

PHOTOGRAPHER. Is that for me?

GRAVEDIGGER. It's to say goodbye and all of the other things I want to say but can't. Because.

FLORIST. A goodbye bouquet. Got it.

> (**THE FLORIST** *makes an elaborate bouquet.*
> **THE PHOTOGRAPHER** *steps out.)*

PHOTOGRAPHER. It seems I'm on a time frame.

GRAVEDIGGER. Put the yellow ones in.

PHOTOGRAPHER. And that death does not take away one's ability to be moved. I'm feeling five distinct feelings. One. Two. Three...no. Just three. Let's move on.

Scene Nine
"The Young Woman and The Young Man"

(Town Green projected on back wall.)

PHOTOGRAPHER. The Town Green.

> (**YOUNG MAN** *enters pulling a child's wagon full of books stacked up, bound together so they reach heights much higher than they otherwise would – almost as tall as the* **YOUNG MAN** *himself.* **YOUNG WOMAN** *enters from opposite direction.)*

YOUNG MAN. Florence, my love.

YOUNG WOMAN. Robert.

PHOTOGRAPHER. Being engaged is a constant. For a short period of time you can say, "my fiancé" this and "my fiancé" that. But sometimes you feel more engaged than other times because being engaged is not a constant.

YOUNG MAN. I'm getting closer, I think. To figuring it all out. They all say a lot of things. About how to be. Some are hard to understand or are not directly applicable. But this is important. I'm going to figure it all out.

PHOTOGRAPHER. The Young Woman doesn't know what to say or how to say it.

YOUNG WOMAN. Robert.

PHOTOGRAPHER. She says.

The Young Woman feels the heavy weight increase, the weight she has been feeling ever since –

> (**YOUNG WOMAN** *collapses.)*

YOUNG MAN. Florence! Are you okay? Help! Help! Hey! Someone!

>*(**EMT 1** and **EMT 2** arrive and go to work. They revive her.)*

EMT 1. Stand back.

EMT 2. Miss? Young Woman, can you hear me?

YOUNG WOMAN. Yes. Sorry. Sorry, everyone.

YOUNG MAN. What's wrong?

EMT 2. Are you okay to sit up?

EMT 1. Drink this.

YOUNG WOMAN. Thank you. I'm fine. I just – I can't do it, Robert.

YOUNG MAN. What?

YOUNG WOMAN. I can't marry you.

EMT 1 & EMT 2. Ohh.

YOUNG MAN. But our love. These books. That ring.

YOUNG WOMAN. I just don't think I can be someone's wife. When you asked, I was so happy, but then the other stuff came. Not just doubt. Not just fear. I felt so lonely. And trapped.

I'm not ready to be in a marriage.

I am not who I will be. Neither are you. We change. Marriage will not solve this.

EMT 1. We've seen this before. My first husband.

EMT 2. My second wife.

YOUNG MAN. But we can change together.

YOUNG WOMAN. I just can't now. There is nothing you can say.

>*(**YOUNG WOMAN** gives him the engagement ring back. **YOUNG MAN** accepts it.)*

YOUNG MAN. I think I need to be alone. Right now. Call me tomorrow.

YOUNG WOMAN. Okay.

YOUNG MAN. Or the day after. Or the day after that. I have a lot of reading to do. I might need different books.

> (**YOUNG MAN** *and* **YOUNG WOMAN** *exit in different directions.*)

> (**EMT 1** *and* **EMT 2** *start to exit. They are offstage or almost offstage for their next lines.*)

EMT 2. You still with that guy?

EMT 1. Yup.

Scene Ten
"The Librarian and The Photographer"

(Graveyard projected. **THE LIBRARIAN** *walks to the grave of* **THE PHOTOGRAPHER.** **THE PHOTOGRAPHER** *watches.)*

PHOTOGRAPHER. So this is happening. At my grave. The Librarian.

LIBRARIAN. Hi. I wanted to… This is hard. I. Well, I guess I came for your blessing? I know we were never what you'd call the best of friends. Not that we – I wanted good things for you. Better than what happened. I mean that. I'm not bitter. I'm not complaining… When I let him go all those years ago. I guess what I'm saying is, I want him back. Which is to say get to know who he has become. But I can't do that if I don't feel like it's okay with you. – What am I saying? He doesn't want me. The love you had was enough for life. Wasn't it? I'm sorry to bother you. Please rest. Peacefully. Sorry.

*(***GRAVEDIGGER*** *has entered during this. He has arms full of flowers.)*

Hi Earl. How's your mother?

GRAVEDIGGER. Good. Good. She crochets now.

LIBRARIAN. When you came in, did you hear me, talking to the gravestone?

GRAVEDIGGER. Oh. Eh. Um. Yup. Yup.

LIBRARIAN. It's silly I know. She can't hear me.

GRAVEDIGGER. She can hear you. The question isn't whether she can hear you.

PHOTOGRAPHER. Stop.

*(***THE GRAVEDIGGER*** *stops speaking.* **PHOTOGRAPHER** *exits, plunging them into*

darkness and walking into her own light and towards the next scene.)

Scene Eleven
"The History Professor and The Mystery Novelist"

(THE PHOTOGRAPHER *walks into the next scene. Harry's Place is projected again.* THE HISTORY PROFESSOR *and* THE MYSTERY NOVELIST *enter while* PHOTOGRAPHER *speaks and they sit at a table.*)

PHOTOGRAPHER. The History Professor and The Mystery Novelist sit in silence.

They miss each other with an ache more painful than when they were first dating. They are both miserable. But he doesn't think she feels the same way. She does. He thinks she loves her empty house. She did. For a day or two. She thinks he loves his bachelor life. He doesn't. They are so desperate it's acidic in their mouths.

HISTORY PROFESSOR. How's the house? If you want, I could come over, take care of some chores. Change a few lightbulbs.

MYSTERY NOVELIST. That would be nice. If it's not too much trouble.

HISTORY PROFESSOR. I don't have to stay long if you don't want.

MYSTERY NOVELIST. It's quiet in the house.

HISTORY PROFESSOR. You like it like that.

MYSTERY NOVELIST. I do. Sometimes. Sorry if I'm keeping you.

HISTORY PROFESSOR. Not at all. How's the novel?

MYSTERY NOVELIST. Getting there. How's the research?

HISTORY PROFESSOR. Frustrating.

(*Beat.*)

I miss you.

PHOTOGRAPHER. She didn't expect that.

MYSTERY NOVELIST. You do? What do you miss?

HISTORY PROFESSOR. Everything.

PHOTOGRAPHER. And he means it. She thinks she might miss everything about him too. Last night she found his fingernail clipping on the rug and almost cried. But she doesn't say that. Instead she says –

MYSTERY NOVELIST. You can move back in if you want.

PHOTOGRAPHER. She surprises herself by saying this.

HISTORY PROFESSOR. I'd like that. Do you mean –?

MYSTERY NOVELIST. On a trial basis. What will we tell the children?

HISTORY PROFESSOR. We'll think of something.

(They kiss.)

Scene Twelve
"The Photographer and The Gravedigger"

(Projection of graveyard. **THE PHOTOGRAPHER** *finds herself there.* **GRAVEDIGGER** *appears. He holds the bouquet of flowers.)*

GRAVEDIGGER. It's time to go – when it's time, it's time. You can feel it, can't you?

PHOTOGRAPHER. But I'm not ready.

GRAVEDIGGER. You can't argue with me about it. I mean it won't do any good. When it's time, it's time.

(He hands her the flowers. She accepts them.)

PHOTOGRAPHER. Thank you, Earl, for...everything.

GRAVEDIGGER. It was nothing.

(She kisses him on the cheek. The buzzing for a second from earlier. Then it's gone.)

PHOTOGRAPHER. There's just one thing I have to do.

*(***THE GRAVEDIGGER*** *looks at her but says nothing. The projection changes. He leaves.)*

Scene Thirteen
"The Photographer and The Hardware Store Owner and The Librarian"

(The Hardware Store is projected.)

(The mirrored ball drops from the ceiling. Light change. Music.* **THE HARDWARE STORE OWNER** *and* **THE LIBRARIAN** *dance close.)*

PHOTOGRAPHER. *(Reacting to the flashback.)* OH!

LIBRARIAN. Promise me we'll be together forever.

HARDWARE STORE OWNER. Okay. I promise.

LIBRARIAN. Even in death?

HARDWARE STORE OWNER. What?

LIBRARIAN. If I die, you'll keep loving me and never love anyone else.

Until we are buried next to each other.

HARDWARE STORE OWNER. Uh.

LIBRARIAN. Just tell me you love me forever and always.

HARDWARE STORE OWNER. I do.

*(***THE PHOTOGRAPHER*** gives the flowers to the* **LIBRARIAN** *now. The lights change. The music* changes.* **THE LIBRARIAN** *and* **THE HARDWARE STORE OWNER** *separate and he begins to dance with the* **PHOTOGRAPHER.** *They are all older now.* **THE LIBRARIAN** *moves outside and watches them through the hardware store window.)*

---

* A license to produce *Kodachrome (One-Act Version)* does not include a performance license for any third-party or copyrighted music. Licensees should create an original composition or use music in the public domain. For further information, please see the Music and Third Party Materials Use Note on page iii.

Suzanne. I knew you were still here. Somehow. I miss you so much it hurts.

PHOTOGRAPHER. Me too, Charlie. I want to know, when I'm gone, you'll be okay. I want you – I want you to go to her.

HARDWARE STORE OWNER. No.

PHOTOGRAPHER. It's what you want too. You're alive. Be alive.

HARDWARE STORE OWNER. *(Starting to come around.)* What if... What if I do it all wrong?

PHOTOGRAPHER. You can't do nothing new and wonder why you're unhappy with your life.

HARDWARE STORE OWNER. *(Accepting.)* I know.

> *(She embraces him, moves away. The lights become normal daytime lights.* **THE LIBRARIAN** *has re-entered. We are in the Hardware Store and* **THE LIBRARIAN** *and* **THE HARDWARE STORE OWNER** *look at each other. Some time has passed but no time has passed.)*

LIBRARIAN. I forgot the lightbulbs.

HARDWARE STORE OWNER. I'm glad you came back. I was thinking about that dinner. I think. I think. I'd really like that. To take you out.

LIBRARIAN. I'd like that.

HARDWARE STORE OWNER. It's been a long time. You're more beautiful now.

> *(He takes her hand and they exit.* **THE PHOTOGRAPHER** *reappears. All the projections we have seen in the play so far flash on the screen super fast, one after*

another. **THE PHOTOGRAPHER** *takes her camera off and places it at her feet.)*

PHOTOGRAPHER. So that's that. It was really nice showing you around. I hope it helped. I only wish we had more time. But I guess... Okay. I have loved.

(Projection: A blank slide – all white light. The lights come up big and full. As bright and as white as possible. It blinds the audience. It envelops **THE PHOTOGRAPHER.** *She raises her arms and looks up. And then Blackout.)*

End of Play

www.ingramcontent.com/pod-product-compliance
Lightning Source LLC
Chambersburg PA
CBHW070403120726
47909CB00008B/2970